Little Bear's Loose Tooth

BY

ELSE HOLMELUND MINARIK

ILLUSTRATIONS BY
CHRIS HAHNER

HarperFestival®
A Division of HarperCollins*Publishers*

One morning when Little Bear
woke up, his mouth felt strange.
When he moved his tongue,
his tooth wiggled.

"My tooth is *looth*," said Little Bear.

He wiggled his tooth with his tongue.

"That is a very loose tooth,"

said Mother Bear.

Little Bear wanted his tooth to fall out.

He wanted to know what

the tooth fairy would bring him.

So Little Bear waited for it to fall out.

After breakfast, Little Bear practiced
whistling with Father Bear.
Then he drew a picture of himself
with a big space in his smile.
Little Bear felt around in his mouth.
His tooth was still there.

Little Bear found Cat, Duck, and Emily
in the field playing with butterflies.
"My tooth is *looth*!" said Little Bear.
Little Bear wiggled his tooth proudly.

His friends wanted to make
Little Bear's tooth fall out.
Duck had an idea.
"Little Bear could hang upside
down from the tree," she said.

Cat, Duck, Emily, and Little Bear
climbed a tall oak.
But it was much too high.
"I'm *dithy*," said Little Bear.

So they climbed down.

Little Bear felt around in his mouth.

The loose tooth was still there.

Emily had an idea.

She took a piece of string

and tied it to Little Bear's tooth.

Then she tied the other end to a rock.

She climbed the big oak again.

14

Emily dropped the rock

from a branch high up

in the big oak.

But the string broke!

The rock fell to the ground, and

Little Bear's tooth hadn't come out.

Owl flew over and asked
what they were doing.
"My tooth is *looth*," said Little Bear.
"We're trying to help Little Bear's
tooth fall out," said Emily.

Owl had an idea.

He whispered in Emily's ear.

Emily ran to get her bike.

Owl tied the string to Emily's bike.

Emily climbed on and pedaled away.

But the string came untied,

and Little Bear still had his tooth.

All of this work had made

Little Bear hungry.

He waved good-bye to his friends

and whistled as he walked home.

That night, Mother Bear made
corn on the cob for dinner.
Little Bear took a big bite.

Little Bear's mouth felt strange.

His tooth had fallen out!

"That's a beauty," said Father Bear.

Little Bear tried to whistle.

He couldn't make a sound!

"My whistle is gone," he said.

"You'll get it back when your

new tooth comes in," said Father Bear.

After dinner, Little Bear brushed

his teeth very carefully.

He brushed the one that fell out, too.

Little Bear wanted it to be nice and

clean for the tooth fairy.

Before bed, Little Bear placed

the tooth under his pillow.

Father Bear whistled

as he tucked him in.

Little Bear tried to whistle back,

but no sound came out.

The next morning,

Little Bear woke very early.

He looked under his pillow

and found a shiny red whistle.

At the breakfast table,

Little Bear whistled happily.

"The tooth fairy knew just

what I wanted," said Little Bear.

After breakfast,

Little Bear went out to find his friends.

He whistled all the way,

and the birds whistled back.